THE MYSTERY OF THE STOLEN NECKLACE

2

THE MYSTERY OF THE STOLEN NECKLACE

Sycamore Street Mysteries #3

By Willow Night

Illustrated by Elizabeth Leach

Table of Contents

Chapter 1... 7

Chapter 2...16

Chapter 3...25

Chapter 4...32

Chapter 5...41

Chapter 6...50

Chapter 7...58

Chapter 8...65

Chapter 9...73

Chapter 10...82

Acknowledgements......................................91

About the Author...92

Chapter 1...93

Look for all the Sycamore Street Mysteries:

The Mystery of the Haunted House

The Mystery of the Toxic Playground

The Mystery of the Stolen Necklace

The Mystery of the Missing Books

The Mystery of the Old Town Hall

Chapter 1

Noah Walker lay on the couch, staring at the ceiling and waiting to blow his nose again. Every year he got sick right at the start of school. His head hurt, and his nose was running.

Outside it was sunny and cool. It was a beautiful day to ride a bike or see what Josh was up to.

Noah reached over and pulled the window open. Fresh air blew in, and he sneezed and blew his nose. He lay back down to look at the ceiling again.

While the cat came over to walk on him, he heard his brother Josh talking to Bill from down the street. Josh wanted to install a zipline in the clubhouse. Mom and Dad said no at first.

Josh asked their neighbor Bill to make a sketch of the plan and talk to their parents about it. Bill could build anything. Their parents finally agreed they could add a zipline to the clubhouse if Bill helped.

Josh's plan to have the zipline run to another tree was out. Apparently, that would lead to a high-speed crash. Bill didn't have a way to make *that* safe.

So they were measuring and getting ready to build by the back gate. If the zipline didn't go to another tree, Josh wanted it to go to the back gate for a quick getaway.

"What do you need to get away from?" Bill asked Josh.

"Oh, you never know," Josh replied.

The brothers had made a few escapes lately. With their friend Olivia, and help from her baby sister Emily, they had solved mysteries and made a few getaways, too.

"Hey!" Noah heard his brother say. He struggled upright to see Olivia pull up on her bike. She was wearing jeans and a T-shirt, and her dark curly hair was in a ponytail under her bike helmet.

Olivia took off her helmet and said hi to Josh. Bill was up in the clubhouse, installing clamps.

"Where's Noah? I have some news," Olivia said, glancing around.

Josh pointed to the house and Olivia looked over. Her eyes met Noah's through the window. Noah gave her a half-hearted wave.

"What's wrong with him?" she asked Josh.

"He's sick. It happens every fall. He goes to school and the next week he gets sick. Mom says

10

it's from getting up early and all the germs at school," Josh told her. "What's your news?"

"Hang on! I want to hear, too," Noah called through the window. He climbed off the couch, feeling cold, and pulled a hoodie over his sweater. Then Noah walked out the back door and over to them.

Olivia raised her eyebrows at Noah all bundled up. "Feeling cold?"

Noah sighed. "I'm sick, okay?" Then he sneezed.

Olivia took a step back. "Okay, don't infect me. I have some news," she added mysteriously.

Bill walked over carrying a couple more clamps.

"How's it going on this end, Josh?" he asked.

Josh had pretty much stopped working. He looked guilty and said, "Olivia just stopped by."

"Hi, Mr. Bill," Olivia greeted him.

"Just Bill is fine," Bill told her. "So are we stopping for today?"

"No," Josh said. "It's just, Olivia said she had …" he stopped, not sure if the news was the kind to share with Bill.

"It's okay," Olivia told Josh. "Bill, I heard that there was a robbery at the hardware shop!"

"A robbery?" Noah asked.

"Did somebody steal power tools?" Bill asked, interested. He was lining up a plank over the top of the gate, which would hold the zipline.

"No, someone stole jewelry from the jewelry repair lady. One was an antique diamond necklace worth thousands of dollars! There's a reward for it!"

Josh looked excited. "A reward? To find a stolen necklace? We should check it out." He ran over to the clubhouse and climbed up the ladder. He was probably going to pack a bag of supplies.

Noah groaned. "That's great, Olivia but I can't go anywhere. I can look online and see if I can find anything out about it."

Olivia nodded. "I might go over to the store and see if they have a flyer or a picture of the necklace."

Bill was listening and looked thoughtful.

"There are a couple things we need for the zipline. I can come too and see what the deal is. There are lots of tools there. It's strange that someone would break in and steal jewelry and leave the tools."

"Necklaces are easier to put in your pocket than power tools," Olivia pointed out.

"I guess you're right," Bill said, as Josh ran up with his backpack strapped to his back. "I didn't even know they did jewelry repair over there."

"Are we going to the hardware shop?" Josh asked.

"We are heading there now," Bill told him. "I need some more screws for this, anyway."

"And I'm going back to the couch," Noah grunted as he went in the house. He sank under a blanket with the laptop. He heard the others getting bikes and helmets ready and heading out.

He opened the computer and started by going to a site for the Sycamore neighborhood. The top post, with dozens of comments already, read:

STOLEN: ANTIQUE DIAMOND NECKLACE!!
REWARD FOR RETURN!!

Chapter 2

Josh felt bad for Noah, who had to stay home sick, but he was excited to find out more about the robbery with Olivia and Bill.

They rode down Sycamore Street and out to the main road. The hardware shop had tools and plants for the fall arranged out front: rakes and leaf blowers, and big pots of bright flowers.

Josh climbed off his bike and Olivia helped him lock it to the pole. Bill was locking his bike and then they all looked at the front.

Under the hardware shop sign were two small signs that said KEYS MADE and JEWELRY REPAIR.

"Do hardware shops usually repair jewelry?" Olivia asked Bill.

"No, but they found someone to work in the back where they make keys and do tool repairs. I think she's new," Bill answered.

Josh thought. If the lady had not been working there long, maybe she was secretly a thief. "Do you think she took the necklace?" he asked the others.

Bill shrugged. "I've never even met her," he replied. "But don't say anything like that to her."

Josh knew enough not to accuse someone of a crime before they even started looking for clues.

He followed the others inside. Josh stopped to look at a dark cat sitting next to the paint cans.

"What's your cat's name?" he asked the lady behind the counter.

"Dusty," the clerk said. "She's friendly, you can pet her."

Josh scratched around Dusty's ears. Then he saw that Olivia and Bill had gone into the back room. He went to find them.

Bill was talking to a man who was making keys with a machine. There was an empty desk with small tools on it but no one else was in the room. Mom came here to get copies made of the house key for when Josh and Noah got back from school.

"I heard you all had some excitement," Bill said to the man.

"What a mess," the man answered. "Everyone's upset. The police don't seem to have much to go on. And the insurance companies are fighting."

"Insurance companies?" Bill asked.

As Josh listened, he looked all around. There was the door that they had come through, that led to the rest of the hardware shop. At the back of the room there was another door. He walked over to look out the window next to that door. He saw the alley behind the hardware shop. There was a dumpster and some trucks parked there.

The man was telling Bill that the insurance companies for the store and the owner of the stolen necklace were arguing about paying for the necklace.

"Someone has to pay for the necklace?" Josh asked Olivia quietly.

"The necklace had insurance. The owner pays the company money, and then if the necklace is lost or stolen the company will pay for it."

"How much money are we talking about?" Bill asked the man, "if you don't mind me asking?"

With a glance at the kids the man said quietly, "One hundred thousand dollars."

Josh and Olivia both froze.

"What?" Bill scoffed, "who would bring a necklace like that to a local hardware shop to be repaired?"

"Well, Melissa locks the jewelry up in a safe back there," the man answered.

"I certainly do," said a woman's voice behind them.

Everyone turned as an older woman came over to the empty desk.

"Every piece that I work on is locked up. The system has always worked."

"Melissa, I know you say that," the key man started slowly.

"This is not my fault!" Melissa snapped at him. "The owner of that necklace did not tell me how much it was worth."

"Couldn't you tell from fixing it?" Olivia asked Melissa.

Melissa sighed. "I should have known. But there are so many fakes out there. I didn't think anyone would bring such a valuable antique into our little shop to repair."

"So you didn't lock it up?" Josh asked Melissa.

"I did lock it up, young man!" she said. "No matter the value, I always keep jewelry locked up when it's not being worked on."

"Was it stolen out of the safe?" Bill asked.

"Well, no," Melissa said, "I had it out. I was finished with a few pieces and I was waiting for them to be picked up."

Melissa glanced toward the back door. "They were back here, and I was in the front of the shop. Someone must have come through the back door and stolen them off my desk."

Melissa refused to talk any more about the robbery. So Josh and Olivia followed Bill to the front of the shop where they paid for the screws for the zipline.

Bill chatted with the owner of the shop. They learned that Melissa had not been working for the shop very long, but the customers liked the work that she did. There weren't many places around where you could get jewelry fixed.

They stepped outside and crunched across the leaves. As they unlocked their bikes, they heard loud voices behind a group of small trees.

"How would I know she was going to leave it out?" a woman cried, upset.

Chapter 3

A man spoke in a low tone. "I know you're upset about your grandmother's necklace. We are doing everything we can to find it, ma'am."

"This is so stressful. I just want the whole thing to be over!" the woman sobbed.

"I understand. You can help us try to find out what happened. Can you find the paperwork for the snowflake necklace? That will help us search for it."

The woman said, "I'll see if I can."

A man in a suit came around the corner of the bushes and walked to a car.

Bill looked at Olivia and Josh. "Sounds like that might be the owner of the necklace?" he asked.

Olivia nodded. "I'm going to talk to her."

"Are you sure?" Josh asked. "She sounds upset."

Olivia shrugged. "There's a reward, are you interested in helping?"

They walked around the bushes to find an older lady sitting on a bench, looking at her phone. She looked up.

"Hello," she said glumly.

Olivia came over. "We were really sorry to hear about your necklace being stolen. We'd like to help find it if we can."

The woman looked surprised. "That's okay, honey, you kids don't have to do that."

"Excuse me, there's a reward, right?" Josh couldn't help asking.

The lady smiled a little. "Oh, I understand."

Josh looked embarrassed.

"I told them about it," Bill said. "I read about it online."

"I think the insurance company set up the reward," she told them.

"Well, is there anything we can do to help?" Olivia asked again.

The woman shrugged. "It's gone. Someone stole it."

"Ma'am, did you check the pawnshops in the area?" Bill asked. "The thief might have gone to resell it right away. That's often what happens."

"No, I haven't," she answered.

"We can help with that," Olivia suggested.

The woman looked from Olivia to Josh to Bill. "Okay. Thank you." She handed Olivia a card. "Here's my number. Let me know if you find it." She got up and walked away.

Olivia looked at the card and then tucked it inside her bag. "She didn't tell us what it looks like."

Bill nodded. "I think there's a picture online. Check that carefully. Do you know how to check the pawnshops?"

Olivia thought. "Well, I can call all the shops in this part of the city and ask if they had anyone come in with a diamond necklace in the last couple of days. If they have and it's close by we can go take a look."

"Sounds like you got this," Bill told her. "I have to go now. Are you two okay riding back alone?"

"Of course!" Josh answered, and Olivia nodded. Bill rode off.

Josh and Olivia decided to have one last look around before they went home. They searched around the front of the store, where the rakes and leaf blowers were set up.

Then, after no one stopped them, they went into the alley behind the shop. The alley stretched all the way up the street, with back doors to the hardware shop, a barbershop, a small bookstore, and doctors' offices at the end of the block.

"Anyone could have come back here and tried the door," Olivia said to Josh.

"Yeah, but how did they know the necklace was in there? And that no one would be in the back room to catch them?"

"I wonder if the employees always watch sports in the front room. They might have known a game was on? That everyone would be in front of the TV?"

They couldn't find anything behind the hardware shop. Josh was going to suggest searching the rest of the alley when a man stepped out of the back door of the barbershop with a bag of garbage for the dumpster.

"Hey!" he called. "What are you kids doing back here?"

Chapter 4

"We're looking for stolen jewelry!" Josh said to the man. Olivia sighed and shook her head.

The man narrowed his eyes and looked around the alley himself. "How did you know about the necklace? Why would it be back here?"

"We saw it posted online," Olivia told him. "And we heard that it was taken by someone who came in through the back door."

"Is that so?" the man asked. "The thief came from back here, eh?" He looked up and down the alley. "Maybe I should start locking the door."

"You don't lock your door?" Josh asked the man.

The man shook his head. "Not during the day. It's so quiet on this block, we've never had a break-in before. Did you check the whole alley?" he asked, starting to poke around. "If the jewelry looked cheap the thief might have just thrown it away."

He cracked the dumpster to peek inside but closed it again. "Stinks," he grunted.

They slowly moved up the alley towards the doctors' offices. Josh and the man looked around the back doors and bins on one side of the alley, and Olivia checked the other side. Suddenly Josh let out a shout.

Olivia dashed over as he pulled a tangle of gold from a recycling bin.

"We found it!" Josh yelled. "We found it, Olivia!"

"Wow," said Olivia. "That was fast. The thief just threw it away?"

"Hey, good work, kids," the man was smiling. "Let's head back and see what they think at the hardware shop!"

They burst through the door to the hardware shop with Josh lifting the pile of jewelry in the air. "We found your jewelry in the trash!"

The store owner blinked at the group. Olivia said that they had been checking the alley behind the store for clues when they found this jewelry in a recycling bin.

"Is this the necklace that was stolen?" Olivia asked. The man from the barbershop listened.

"Go check with Melissa," the owner told them.

The kids ran to the back room. Melissa and the man who made keys looked up from their desks. Josh plopped the tangled jewelry down in front of her.

"We found this in the alley," he told her. "Is this the necklace that was taken?"

Melissa's eyes widened as she sorted through the pile. With a smile she said, "Good work! Thank you, I can't believe it."

But her face fell as she finished pulling the necklaces apart from each other.

"But where is the diamond necklace? Is this all there was?"

Josh and Olivia looked for a diamond snowflake necklace, but it was true, they didn't see anything like a diamond.

Melissa thought for a moment. "The thief must have known what he was looking for. I don't know how. Thank you for bringing me these. They aren't valuable, but I'm sure the owners will be happy to get them back."

Olivia and Josh rode to Olivia's house where they ate sandwiches that Olivia threw together. She told Josh, "It feels like I'm babysitting you."

"Hey!" Josh said. "I don't need a babysitter. I'll clean up." And he did.

Together they went to Olivia's room to look up pawnshops.

"But what is a pawnshop? Does it sell chess pieces?" Josh asked.

"No," Olivia laughed. "People sell their stuff to a pawnshop for money, or they can get a loan from a pawnshop in return for their jewelry or other stuff."

"What happens to their stuff?" Josh asked.

"Either you come back and repay the loan and get your stuff back or the pawnshop sells it for a profit."

"Why don't people just sell their things on the internet?" Josh asked.

"I think a lot of people do these days," Olivia answered. She was making a list of shop names and phone numbers on her tablet.

"Why don't you call Noah and have him see if the necklace is for sale on eBay or Craigslist?"

Josh ran off to call his brother. Olivia looked at her list of shops. There were five, and they were all within two miles of the hardware shop. That was as far as she wanted to search right now.

She put on a Bluetooth headset and started making calls, adding notes to her list. After she had talked to people in all five shops, she crossed off two, as they'd had no jewelry come in for over a week. The other three did, including necklaces.

Olivia found the addresses and studied a route, deciding which way to go first.

Then she joined Josh in the kitchen to make a plan. They looked at the tablet to see where the three stores were.

"So, someone could steal the necklace and take it to a pawnshop to sell right away?"

"Yes ...." Olivia trailed off. "It doesn't seem like they would get a lot of money from that."

"After all, it was real diamonds, but they wouldn't have any proof. Melissa said *she* hadn't even known how valuable it was. How would a thief or a pawnshop owner know?" she asked.

Josh didn't know. He reported that Noah would try to find any valuable diamond necklaces that were put up for sale online in the last couple of days.

Since they didn't have anything else to do, they got some supplies including a camera to take pictures of any necklaces they found and set off to visit all the pawnshops.

Chapter 5

Despite a cool breeze, the sun was hot on Josh's back as he rode his bike down a side street behind Olivia. Olivia had the address of the pawnshop, but she had never been there before. Josh had never been to any kind of pawnshop.

When they got to the block, they rode around to the main road. They walked their bikes, reading the addresses until they got to the number they were looking for.

It was a crumbling brick building with peeling paint on the windows. It said 523 in big numbers, but there was no sign of the shop.

Olivia pulled out her phone to double-check the address.

"Should be 523. Here, hold this a second." She ran up the steps to try the door of the brick building. It was locked. She looked down at Josh, holding the bikes.

They checked to see if there was another door. There was a mattress store on one side of the building and on the other side was a gas station. The gas station had an open garage door and a car was getting fixed.

Josh felt confused.

"Where's the shop?" he asked.

"Let's check around back, I guess?" Olivia suggested. They walked their bikes past the gas station and entered the alley behind. The alley was dirty and there was garbage overflowing out of garbage cans behind the brick building at 523.

A rustle behind a garbage can was probably a rat, Josh thought.

Past the garbage cans was a door, with a sign next to it that read:

HONEST PAWN AND JEWELRY
KNOCK AND RING THE BELL

Trying not to breathe through her nose, Olivia pushed the doorbell and knocked loudly on the door. Josh jumped.

"It's okay," she told him, a little unsure.

"I know," he said. He held tight onto the handlebars. "What should we do with the bikes?"

Olivia looked around. She didn't think it was a good idea to leave them in this alley. She was about to suggest they go around front to find a place to lock them up when the door was yanked open by a man who filled the whole doorway.

Olivia looked up at the man, who was very tall, with a bushy beard. He was wearing a baseball cap and a big grey hoodie.

"Hi," she squeaked. "I'm looking for Honest Pawn and Jewelry."

The man nodded.

"I'm Olivia," she added. "Did we talk on the phone?"

The man answered in a deep voice, "You called about the necklace?"

Olivia nodded. Josh said to the man, "Is there a place we can put our bikes?"

The man looked behind him. "Here, come in," he said. "You can use the hallway; the door is always locked."

They rolled their bikes through the door into an empty hallway, painted white with long, bright lightbulbs on the ceiling that hurt Josh's eyes.

"Do your parents know you're here?" the man asked as they followed him to the door of his shop.

"Yes, my mom knows," Olivia answered. They let Olivia's mom know all the shops they would be visiting. Josh shrugged. His parents knew he was with Olivia, and that was good enough for them.

"Okay. Come in, I can show you the jewelry that came in this week."

They stepped into the shop. There was a woman sitting on a folding chair and a couple of teenagers looking at guitars in a glass case. The shop was very crowded with all kinds of stuff.

Josh saw a case behind the counter with guns of different sizes. Another counter held jewelry and watches. All around the small room were computers, power tools, video games, and musical instruments.

Josh followed Olivia to the jewelry counter. But the man waved them over to the checkout counter. He went into a back room and came back with a box.

"Those pieces are for sale, but these are the recent ones. Can't sell them for thirty days."

Inside the box were sparkling gold and silver watches as well as earrings, bracelets and rings.

The shop owner pulled out a second box and opened it to reveal a neat row of necklaces.

"Now, you kids understand I can't release anything to you without a police report," the man told them sternly.

"We understand, thank you. We're just helping the owner check the shops in case the thief pawned the necklace right away." Olivia pulled her tablet out of her bag. "This is a picture of the diamond necklace that was stolen."

She showed the tablet to the man and he bent down to take a look. The necklace had a thin gold chain and a pendant that was shaped like a snowflake. Each part of the snowflake was a glittering diamond.

They turned to the box with the necklaces. There were some with diamonds, but none had a snowflake pendant. Josh went over to the jewelry case and came back.

"Nothing over here," he said.

Olivia nodded and pulled out her tablet, swiping a big X over HONEST PAWN AND JEWELRY in their list.

Chapter 6

Late in the afternoon Josh and Olivia were tired, hungry and thirsty after riding their bikes for the whole afternoon checking the pawnshops.

Although the shops were interesting, none of them had a snowflake necklace that looked like the stolen necklace.

Olivia looked tired as she said goodbye. Noah came out of the house, wrapped in a thick sweater, to say that he hadn't seen anything online.

"Call me in the morning and let me know if you guys find anything. Not sure what the next move is," she admitted. "You could ask your parents what they've heard."

Noah looked tired and sick. "Maybe I'll have an idea in the morning. I can't think right now—my head doesn't feel great."

"I'm sorry," Olivia said. "You should sleep. I hope you feel better."

"I'll see if Bill thought of anything," Josh told them. The two sixth graders looked a little hopeful at this.

"Good idea!" Olivia told him. "Okay, good night."

The boys went in to help with dinner. Noah went straight to bed, so Josh ate tacos with Mom and Dad and helped clean up. He didn't have a way to research the necklace online, so he played cards with his parents until it was time to go to bed.

In the morning Noah woke up feeling better. He took a shower and blew his nose about twenty times. Then he felt much better and went to the kitchen to look for breakfast.

Josh came in and as they had eggs and toast, he told Noah about finding the jewelry in the alley, but not the necklace. And then going to pawnshops—with Olivia—and still not finding anything.

"Melissa and the man from the barbershop both thought that the thief must have known what they were looking for. But how would they know which necklace was the valuable one?" Josh asked his brother.

Noah wasn't sure. But after breakfast was cleaned up he grabbed his laptop.

"Homework?" Mom asked, wandering through.

"I'm helping someone look for something they lost," Noah said.

"Okay," Mom answered. "I'm glad you're feeling better."

"I'm feeling a lot better," he told Mom.

She gave him a little hug and kissed the top of his head. Noah waited until she left and then opened a couple of tabs including eBay and Craigslist to search for the words *diamond*, *snowflake*, and *necklace*.

There was nothing on eBay, but on Craigslist the search showed a result! There was a headline "Antique Diamond Snowflake

Necklace" and a description next to the price of $100,000. There was a picture that looked exactly like the diamond snowflake necklace they were looking for!

Noah clicked for more information and Josh grabbed the phone right away to call Olivia.

Olivia was able to find the same post within seconds. She took screenshots of it. There was no name or phone number. The only way to contact the person was to email them through Craigslist.

"I'll dig around and see if I can find this posted anywhere else," Olivia said. "Then we can call the owner and let her know!"

Since Noah was still feeling tired, Olivia rode her bike to Sycamore Street once she had found out everything she could about the post about the necklace.

When Olivia arrived, they called the owner of the necklace on Olivia's cell phone. Olivia was excited to tell her about the post they had found.

"It's up on Craigslist right now! I think the police can get a warrant to check out this post and find out the IP address and identity of the poster," Olivia told her.

"Oh! That's great! Can they do that?" the owner asked.

"And if you want," Noah added, "we can write back to the post and see if the thief will make a plan to meet us and sell us the necklace."

"Oh no," the woman exclaimed. "That sounds really dangerous. You kids shouldn't be getting involved with a thief."

"Thank you so much for letting me know about this post," she went on. "I will pass this information on. I really must insist that you do not get involved with a criminal on my behalf."

"Okay," Noah replied, a little disappointed. They brought the owner up to date about Josh's discovery of the stolen jewelry and the pawnshops they had checked.

"Wow, you are working very hard. I think this will be plenty for the police to go on."

"Do you want us to send these screenshots to the police?" Olivia asked. She was disappointed that the owner didn't want more help after they had made several big discoveries.

"No, thank you," the owner of the necklace replied. "I'll take care of that."

Moments after they got off the phone, Noah was looking at his laptop, double-checking the post on Craigslist selling the necklace.

"Hey guys," he called to the others. "The post is gone!"

Chapter 7

Olivia and Josh ran over to look over Noah's shoulder. He searched for "snowflake diamond" and then for "snowflake necklace" and then for "antique diamond necklace." Nothing came up.

"That's funny," Olivia said quietly.

"What is?" Josh wanted to know.

"Well," Olivia answered, "we just discovered the post. And then it gets taken down right away."

Olivia pulled her tablet out of her messenger bag and looked at the pictures she had taken of the post. The date showed it had only been put up this morning, about an hour earlier.

"Maybe they already found someone to buy it?" Josh asked.

"For one hundred thousand dollars?" Noah was skeptical. "I think it would take a long time to find someone who wanted to spend that much money on a necklace off of Craigslist. Olivia is it possible the thief could tell we discovered the post?"

"I don't see how..." Olivia trailed off. She glanced around. "Do you think your family is being spied on?"

"No, we are so low tech," Josh complained.

"Very unlikely," Noah agreed.

They talked about whether to send the screenshots to the police.

"I'm not sure there's a lot they can do now that the post is taken down," Olivia said.

Noah thought they should walk back over to the hardware shop and search the alley again. Then as Noah kept searching for "snowflake" and "diamond" and "necklace" he shouted again as something new came up.

Antique Star Diamond Necklace $95,000

The picture was the same as the snowflake necklace!

"It does kind of look like a star," Josh said.

"The thief must think we are really stupid," Noah said, shaking his head.

"But Noah, how could they know it was us?" Olivia was getting frustrated.

"Tell you what," Noah said. "Let's send an email asking about the necklace—see if we can find anything out?"

Olivia gave a nervous smile. "The owner said that was too dangerous."

"Who cares?" said Josh. "If she gets her necklace back. And we get the reward."

They all went to sit on the couch, with Noah in the middle and the laptop on his lap. Olivia clicked around on her tablet, screenshotting the new post about the "star" necklace.

Noah clicked on "reply" and his email program opened. He wrote this note:

Hello. I'm interested in the star necklace for sale on Craigslist. Is it still for sale? Is there a time I can see the necklace in person?

"Hang on," Olivia said. "Is that your regular school email? We'd better use an anonymous address." She took the laptop and cut and pasted Noah's email into a site to send it from a random phone number.

They all looked at each other and nodded, and Olivia hit the send button. She had set it up to text her phone when there was a reply.

"Now what?" Josh asked.

They decided to ride over to the hardware shop to get out of the house and see if there was any news about the necklace. It was a clear fall day and the leaves were turning bright orange and red on the trees as they rode by.

Inside the hardware shop they went in the back to talk to Melissa.

Melissa was talking to a man who looked familiar.

"I don't think there's anything else I can tell you about that day," she was saying to him.

"Well, thank you for your time," the man said.

The man walked out, and Melissa looked upset.

"Is everything okay?" Noah asked politely.

Melissa sighed. "It's just the insurance company. They want me to pay a lot more money now that there's been a robbery here."

"But it's not your fault!" Olivia said.

"I know," Melissa replied. "But they don't care."

Suddenly Olivia's phone dinged. The kids tensed. It might be a message from the thief!

"We'll let you know if we hear anything!" Olivia promised as they hurried out of the store.

Chapter 8

Outside Olivia pulled out her phone and they crowded around it. The message was an answer from the Craigslist posting. It read:

The necklace is available. I can meet today at noon.

Olivia gulped. "It's 11:30 now!" she said. She quickly typed back:

I can meet at noon in the Sycamore neighborhood. At Charlie's Coffee and Cafe?

The kids looked at each other nervously.

"This doesn't seem safe," Josh said.

"We can peek in and take pictures from the outside," Olivia said. "And we don't have to go at all. Maybe he won't answer."

But just then her phone dinged again, and the answer came:

Ok. See you then.

"Well?" Olivia asked. "Should we go over to Charlie's Cafe?" She checked her bag for her phone and wallet.

They climbed on their bikes and rode to Charlie's Coffee and Cafe. They usually came here for cookies or a muffin and locked their bikes to the bike rack in front of the outdoor seating.

Today they stopped a block away by a little grocery store and locked their bikes up there, next to a dog who was waiting for his owner to come out of the grocery.

Josh gave the dog a pat and then the three of them started walking up the block towards the corner with the cafe.

"How will we know who the thief is?" Noah asked.

"Let's scout it out first," Olivia said. "I'll take pictures. If nothing else, we can use facial recognition to look up some names."

Josh looked at Olivia. "Wow," he said. "You are, like, really a spy. It's a little scary."

Olivia smiled. "You guys are safe with me. We should stop talking about this now."

Noah and Josh sat on a bench and drank from their water bottles while Olivia took out her camera and pretended to take pictures of the buildings and trees on the block, including the building with Charlie's Coffee and Cafe in the basement.

There were several people sitting at tables out front. One man was a dog walker. He was sitting with four small dogs on leashes, giving them treats while he drank coffee.

A couple of college students sat with their laptops, and a group of people all sat together with yoga mats.

"I don't think it's any of them," Noah said to Olivia as she came to sit down.

"Yeah," agreed Olivia. "I'm going to go in."

"I don't know, Olivia," Noah said.

"You can do it," encouraged Josh.

"I'll use my phone and pretend to take selfies in the cafe," Olivia suggested.

"That doesn't sound legal to me," Noah argued.

"I'm doing it to help catch the thief. I'm not going to use the pictures for anything else," said Olivia.

Just then a man walked out of the cafe. He had a long coat on, and a baseball cap and he looked all around and then walked quickly up the hill.

"What if that was him?" Olivia asked.

"Should we follow him?" said Josh.

Olivia checked her phone. It was just turning twelve o'clock now. "He probably wouldn't be leaving so soon, it's just noon now."

"Unless he suspected us," Noah added.

"Look, I'll just order a hot chocolate and come back out." She took her phone and wallet out of her bag and stuck them in her jeans pocket. She handed her bag to Josh and Noah. "Take care of this, okay?"

They watched as Olivia looked both ways and crossed the street, pulling her phone out of her pocket.

Noah shivered even though it was warm with the sun shining on them. He suggested petting the dogs, so they crossed the street and said hi to the dog walker.

From where they were standing, they could see through the window into the cafe. Olivia was standing in a short line in front of a counter. There were several people sitting alone at tables.

"It could be any of them," Noah said to his brother in a low voice.

Olivia was holding her phone in line, pretending to take selfies.

"She must be taking pictures of the people. She's pretty good at that!" Josh said to his brother as they moved away from the dog walker, still holding Olivia's bag. Olivia got to the counter and ordered.

As she waited for her order, she turned all the way around for the first time to look in the back of the shop. As they watched, Olivia suddenly looked shocked, said something to the man behind the counter, and ran out the door.

Chapter 9

"Come on, let's get out of here!" she called as she ran towards their bikes.

"Wait! Olivia! What happened?" Noah called.

"Yeah, what about the hot chocolate?" Josh asked.

Olivia kept running until they got to the bikes. She was trying to undo the bike lock that was locking their bikes to the pole.

Noah helped pull the chain off the bikes, panting, "Too much running, why do we always end up running?"

They climbed on their bikes. By now they trusted Olivia. If she said they needed to take off, they would do that. It had happened before.

They rode fast up the block and made their way back to the Walker home on Sycamore Street. Inside the back gate they dropped their bikes and followed Olivia up into the clubhouse.

She grabbed one of Josh's granola bars and dug in. "I'm so hungry all of the sudden," she said.

"Wait, what? Is that why we just ran away from Charlie's Cafe?" Josh asked.

"It *is* getting to be lunch time," Noah remarked as he grabbed one as well. "Well, Olivia? Who was in there? What did you see?"

Olivia's eyes widened. "I don't understand what's going on," she said, pulling out her phone and opening up the pictures. "Take a look."

Josh and Noah bent over the phone as Olivia swiped through a couple of pictures. There was a picture of a man's back as he stood in front of a table. Then there was a picture as the man moved aside. Sitting at the table was the owner of the necklace!

In the picture, the old lady sat alone at the table, clutching her purse and looking nervously out the window.

"What is going on?" Olivia demanded. "Is she a thief? Was she trying to meet the thief?"

"Oh!" Noah said as he remembered something. "I think she is the thief. It's about the insurance."

"What?" Josh asked. "Why would she steal her own necklace?"

Olivia nodded. "She wants the insurance money *and* the money from the sale."

"Hey guys, what is going on?" Josh demanded. "What do you mean?"

Noah explained their theory to Josh as they walked to the hardware shop.

The woman must have come in through the back door and taken her own necklace, then reported it stolen to the police and the insurance company.

"She wants to collect one hundred thousand dollars from the insurance company," Olivia said. "I guess she's trying to sell it and get even more money."

"Pretty dishonest," Noah decided.

"But is it against the law to steal your own necklace?" Josh asked, confused.

"It's fraud to lie like that. I guess we should tell the insurance company. Let's ask Melissa."

They arrived at the hardware shop and walked to the back room where Melissa was working, and the key man was cutting someone's key.

They waited a minute until the loud sound of the key cutting was over and the customer left with her new keys.

"Excuse me," Noah said to Melissa, the jewelry repair woman.

"Yes?" she asked, looking up. Recognizing them she added, "Oh, hello. Thank you again for finding the necklaces that were taken last week. I can't believe they were just thrown out in the alley."

"You're welcome. Actually, we have some information on the snowflake diamond necklace," Olivia told her.

"The owner of the necklace was the thief!" Josh burst out. "She just wanted to get the money from the insurance!"

"That's a very serious thing to say," Melissa said. "What makes you say that?" She came over as Olivia pulled her phone out.

Olivia showed Melissa the screenshot from the two postings on Craigslist advertising the sale of the necklace. Melissa didn't need to look twice.

"That's the necklace," she agreed.

Then they showed her pictures of the texts and the owner of the necklace waiting in the coffee shop at the same time and place that they had arranged with the thief.

"It doesn't really prove it," the key man said.

Melissa looked thoughtful. "I think it's enough that we should let the insurance man know. Do you want to talk to him, or do you want me to talk to him?" she asked Olivia.

The kids glanced at each other. Noah answered, "If you don't mind, we can send you this stuff and you can talk to him. If he needs to speak to us, we're more than happy to, but he's more likely to listen to you, if you know what I mean."

Melissa nodded. "Okay. Send me the pictures you just showed me and screenshots of the texts, all right?"

Olivia started typing on her phone.

"Will the lady go to jail?" asked Noah.

Melissa smiled and shook her head. "I don't think so. It's not a crime to steal your own stuff or try to sell it. They just won't give her the insurance money. And I won't repair any of her jewelry again. I wonder if you'll get the reward?"

Chapter 10

The next morning was cool and crisp and after breakfast Mom and Dad hauled the boys out to help rake the yard. A lot of leaves had come down overnight.

The piles of leaves grew bigger and bigger. Josh was starting to get distracted when Olivia came by on her bike.

"Hi, Mr. and Mrs. Walker," she said. "Can I borrow Josh and Noah for a minute?"

"Oh sure," Dad replied. "I have to go find the yard bags anyway," he called, heading into the garage.

Olivia showed them a message she had gotten back from Melissa. It said that things were all set with the insurance and they had ruled against the claim, meaning they would not pay the money out for the necklace. It also said since the necklace was not stolen, there would be no reward paid out.

"No reward?" Josh asked, disappointed.

"No," Olivia said. "But Melissa's cleared, and she doesn't get in any trouble or have to pay a lot of extra money."

"Josh," she asked, noticing the handle dangling in the doorway. "What's up with the zipline? Is it ready?"

"Almost, we're going to put a bumper at the bottom, so you don't get such a jolt hitting the end. Bill dropped it off, but I probably need his help to install it."

Josh picked up the bumper and they climbed down and went to the end of the zipline to take a look.

"Do you still need help?" Noah asked his parents, who were scooping leaves into bags.

"No, we're almost done," Mom said.

"Hello!" they heard as Bill came around from the alley. "Everyone's out today."

"Hi, Bill," Dad replied. "Just trying to get things cleaned up now that most of the leaves are down off the trees."

"Never-ending battle," Bill shook his head.

"I heard they got everything worked out down at the hardware shop," he said to Mom and Dad.

"Oh, did they find the stolen necklace?" Mom asked.

"I guess it wasn't really stolen," Bill replied. "The owner was just trying to get the insurance money." He looked at Noah, Josh and Olivia and smiled. "The hardware shop people said you all were a big help!"

"Really?" Dad exclaimed. "These guys? They barely got one pile of leaves raked!" he teased.

"Bill, can we finish the zipline now?" asked Josh.

"Sure, buddy," Bill replied, and started hooking up the bumper to the end of the zipline. When it was done, they ran the handle back and forth a couple of times.

Mom looked concerned. "And we're all sure this can hold the kids' weight and they'll be safe?"

"Mom, it's fine," Josh assured her.

"It's secure, that's for sure," Bill said. "But they'll have to hold the handle tight."

Josh climbed up to the platform outside the treehouse and everyone stopped to watch him. He stood at the edge, gripped the handle tightly, and jumped off with a shout. Josh whooshed down to the bottom and bumped gently as his feet reached the ground right at the back gate.

"Wow! Awesome!" Noah said and climbed up to try.

"It's pretty cool," Dad agreed. "Thanks for your help, Bill."

"Oh, no problem at all," Bill replied. "I've got to run over to the hardware shop for a couple things I'm working on today. See you all later."

Noah, Josh and Olivia did the zipline over and over until their arms felt numb from holding themselves up with the handle.

Then they went in and had some apple cider that Mom had warmed up.

"I was actually thinking about walking down to Charlie's Cafe to get lunch. Are you guys interested in coming along?" she asked.

"Yes!" Josh answered. "I'm starving."

"I guess I can leave my homework for after lunch," Noah agreed.

"Thank you, Mrs. Walker," said Olivia.

"Okay, make sure you have a coat in case we want to sit outside," Mom called as she got her purse together.

They followed Mom out the door and started down the hill for Charlie's Coffee and Cafe. And this time all they had to do was eat lunch and get a cookie.

The End

Look for all the Sycamore Street Mysteries:

The Mystery of the Haunted House

The Mystery of the Toxic Playground

The Mystery of the Stolen Necklace

The Mystery of the Missing Books

The Mystery of the Old Town Hall

If you enjoyed this book, please take a few
moments to write a review.

Thank you!

Acknowledgements

I'd like to thank Charley, Naftali, Kiva and Laser. I'd like to thank my parents and Charley's parents for their love and support along the way. Thank you to my editor Rose Green who knows what it sounds like to cut a key.

Thank you to my proofreader Linda Wobus who reads mysteries on her back porch.

Thank you especially to my illustrator Elizabeth Leach for lending her time and talents to this series and bringing Noah, Josh and Olivia to life in her drawings!

About the Author

Willow Night lives in a neighborhood with many necklaces, but none of them have a snowflake diamond pendant.

from *The Mystery of the Missing Books*....

Chapter 1

It was a Monday and it was cold. Outside it wasn't night yet, but Noah knew it would be dark even before dinner time.

In the kitchen it was warm and smelled great. Mom was making chocolate cupcakes. Everyone in the family had been into cupcakes lately. It warmed up the house and made the snow and the cold seem not as bad.

Noah liked cupcakes fine. But Noah's little brother Josh was obsessed with cupcakes. He had decided that cupcakes were his good luck food to eat before climbing. And in the winter Josh went to the climbing gym almost every day.

Mom was getting tired of making cupcakes all the time.

"I think it's time for you to start making these yourself if you really need them," she told Josh as they got ready to frost the cupcakes.

"I don't know how!" Josh argued. "And yours are so good," he added with a winning smile.

Mom smiled back but she told Josh he could learn with the recipe.

"If I had a phone, I could look up cupcake recipes all day," Josh pointed out. A lot of kids in his class had their own phones, but Mom and Dad were waiting until he was a teenager!

"Who would ever think you would need a phone to cook?" Mom asked, laughing. "A bowl, yes, butter, yes, a spoon and a baking sheet. But a phone?"

Noah and Josh spread frosting on the cupcakes. Josh wanted to lay in a good supply of cupcakes before a climbing competition that he had on Friday.

Josh didn't win most of the climbing competitions that he did, but he liked going anyway. Every now and then he had a really good day and got to bring home a trophy.

Noah thought it was just an excuse to go crazy over cupcakes.

The cat came in and crouched next to the table, getting ready to jump up.

"No way!" Josh told the cat. "Stay away from my cupcakes!"

"Where is this recipe from anyway?" Noah asked Mom.

Mom checked her phone and said the name of a new cookbook for cakes and cupcakes. "You can see if they have it at the library. Then you can take over this cupcake stuff. I'm running out of energy to make cupcakes and there's a lot more of winter left!"

Noah wrote the name of the book down. "I need to stop by the library, anyway, do you want to go with me?" he asked his brother.

It was cold outside, and Noah knew Josh would want to avoid going back out. But the thought of cupcakes won out.

"Okay," his little brother agreed. "After I eat a cupcake," he added with a side look at Mom. She rolled her eyes.

"Do you know where your wallet is with your library card?" she asked.

"Yeah, it's in my room."

Noah and Mom both snorted. Josh collected stuff, mostly things to help him prepare for his missions, and his room was packed with stuff. Since it was so cold outside Josh had moved all of the supplies he usually kept in the clubhouse into the house.

But Mom and Dad didn't want the dining room table covered with binoculars and ropes and granola bars. "Where will I play Yahtzee?" Dad had asked. So, Josh had to cram it all in his room.

"I know it's up there! I can find it." Cramming the last bit of cupcake into his mouth, Josh ran out of the room and pounded up the stairs.

Dad walked in with a bag. "Did I hear someone is going over to the library?" he asked. "I have these books to donate."

"We can drop them off," Noah said. "How do you do that?"

"There's a bin around back in the alley, a big bin that says, 'Books to Donate' on the side," Dad answered.

"Got it," Noah agreed and took the books.

"And see you if you can find any of the mysterious, missing books. That's right up your alley," Mom said in an offhand voice.

"What missing books?" Josh said, bursting back into the kitchen with his wallet in his hand and a backpack full of who knows what.

"Well," Dad said, looking over at Mom. She shrugged.

"I think they're having a problem at the library. Getting their book shipments stolen."

"Are they still missing some?" Mom asked, looking concerned.

Dad shook his head. "From what Bill said, they are trying to get more security. But with a public library, you have to apply for funding. Things have gotten better, but they are still missing almost half of their new books."

"Someone is stealing books from the library?" Josh asked. "But the books don't even cost money!"

"Not the books inside the library, Josh," Mom explained. "Libraries buy new books to add to the system when they come out. Like the cake and cupcake cookbook!"

"New books are expensive," Dad pointed out. "And when they get shipped to the library, the boxes are missing from outside and inside the library! It's possible there's just some kind of mix up happening."

Josh and Noah looked at each other. Now they were even more interested in heading over to the library.

Coming out in 2021:
The Mystery of the Missing Books

Made in the USA
Middletown, DE
24 November 2020